Short Afternoons

By the same author

Poetry

Treble Poets One (with Elizabeth Maslen and Stephen Miller)
The Bear Looked Over the Mountain
Bump-Starting the Hearse
The Day Room
Poems 1974–1983

For Children

Rabbiting On
Arthur's Family
Hot Dog
Professor Potts in Africa
Cat Among the Pigeons

As Editor

Soundings
Poems for 9-Year-Olds and Under
Poems for Over-10-Year-Olds

SHORT AFTERNOONS

Kit Wright

HUTCHINSON
London Sydney Auckland Johannesburg

Some of these poems were first broadcast on the BBC World Service, Radio 3 *New Premises* and *Poetry Now* and some first published in the anthologies *First and Always, Poems for Wolfie, Neighbours*, *Poetry Book Society Supplement 1983*, and PEN *New Poetry 1986–7*, and others in *Poetry Review*. To the producers and editors concerned acknowledgement is due.

This edition first published in 1989 by Hutchinson

Century Hutchinson Ltd, Brookmount House,
62–65 Chandos Place, London WC2N 4NW

Century Hutchinson Australia (Pty) Ltd
20 Milsons Point, Sydney, NSW 2061, Australia

Century Hutchinson New Zealand Limited
PO Box 40–086, Glenfield, Auckland 10, New Zealand

Century Hutchinson South Africa (Pty) Ltd
PO Box 337, Bergvlei, 2012 South Africa

British Library Cataloguing in Publication Data
Wright, Kit
Short afternoons.
I. Title
821′.914

ISBN 0–09–173607–2

Phototypeset in Linotron Times by
Input Typesetting Ltd, London
Printed and bound in Great Britain by
Courier International, Tiptree, Essex

To the memory of Dick Johnson 1946–85

'To be at all is to be wrong'
Randall Jarrell

'Come on, big boy,
Ten cents a dance!'
Rogers and Hart

Contents

Sonnet for Dick

My friend looked very beautiful propped on his pillows.
Gently downward tended his dreaming head,
His lean face washed as by underlight of willows
And everything right as rain except he was dead.
So brave in his dying, my friend both kind and clever,
And a useful Number Six who could whack it about.
I have described the man to whomsoever
The hell I've encountered, wandering in and out
Of gaps in the traffic and Hammersmith Irish boozers,
Crying, where and why did Dick Johnson go?
And none of the carloads and none of the boozer users,
Though full up with love and with cameraderie, know
More than us all-of-his-others, assembled to grieve
Dick who, brave as he lived things, took his leave.

Mrs Duffy's Roulade

In the kingdom of the blind everybody's as blind as a bat.
In the kingdom of the drunk everybody's as pissed as a rat.
In the kingdom of the daft everyone's as mad as a hatter
And what's the matter
With that? It's why
In the one-eyed kingdom everybody's got one eye,
Why the days sing helplessly on with the caught bird in their throat
And this land of strangers is stranger than a nine bob note.

A Pastoral Disappointment

Habitate the heart's allotment!
  Tuber-lonesome, earth your doubt
Where the mild potato flowers
  By the peaceful brussels sprout
And the sea-green vegetation
  Calmly washes in and out
    Of light and shade:
A bird sings on the handle of a spade.

Put your shoulder to the silence,
  Bend the buttock to the stoop
Of the creosoted tool-shed.
  See the sweet pea loop the loop
Up the trellis. In due season
  And due order dress the troop
    Of lettuce heads.
Command a rainfall to refresh the beds.

Peace is in the heart's allotment.
  Where the sun has pressed its thumbs,
Tamping down transplanted neighbours,
  Are no mansions, nor are slums,
But an even-handed empire
  Where impartial kindness comes
    To each green thing:
A cabbage white could be this kingdom's king.

But wait! Garrotted in the bindweed,
  Who is this strip-farmer dead?
Slugs exploring either nostril,
  Eye-bulbs bursting from his head?
Hell is in the heart's allotment,

From the green veins gouting red
And its flames
Leaping in the bonfire's funeral games.

Mulch him down and fork him over,
Turn his body through the light
Into mould of under darkness
Where a rooted appetite
Works an income from his liver,
Builds a star upon his night.
Nature's art
And hell's compose the compost of the heart.

Old Hands

(The offices of the National Secular Society and its journal)

On the Holloway Road a short block west of death,
Upstairs old men are disrobing God
And licking envelopes.

High blue veins are in their mottled hands
That pack the *Freethinker*, their tongues
Are rough with love of the cause.

Like King, they have a dream.
Like the tugging summer wind outside,
A vocation.

And they seem kind as they are old,
These volunteer Home Guardsmen
In the army of

Anti-

Christendom, clitorectomy,
Hindu *suttee*, Buddhist corpse-rustlers,
Evangelical thugs and racketeers,

Damnation terrorists
For skies of money. I leave
The creaking office peeling in the sun

For the Broad Street line, ride westward
To meet my mother by the trees by the spire
By the river. She

Was once described as 'the kindest woman in Westerham'.
She'll be on her knees, weeding the churchyard
With the same hands as theirs.

Correspondence

1. Letter to the TLS

Dear Sir:
    I'm preparing a study
Of Blake's Prophetic Books
Provisionally entitled:
BUSINESS REPLY ENVELOPE.
It's a new tack. It might well fail.
I need all the help I can get.
So come on, readers,
Bung in the old suggestions
For cash on the nail
To:
                Arthur Daft, Professor
                Of Singular Studies,
University of Wale

2. Postcard to an Author

Dear Greene:
    I understand you're writing a novel
About this chap who gets into lots of scrapes.
It sounds like a damned good idea to me.
I was wondering whether you'd care to discuss it
Over a bottle of plonk or two or three
Or a hell of a lot of beers
In your Antibes local. I'll be over all summer
And somebody gave me your number. Cheers!

3. Sea Missive

Dear Voice:
    I heard you reading the Shipping Forecast
Yesterday afternoon and enjoyed it
Even more than usual.
                                        My bark, I may say,
Is far from ship-shape, backing northotherwise,
Poor to appalling . . . good,

Therefore, to be airwave-worthy,
And navigate not by your pinpoints
But by your encouraging tone
Alone:

For I have no bearings at all in this cliff-high sea
And when I go down off Rockall or Malin
Or Dogger or Finisterre,
The giant salt boon of your presence there
Will more than compensate
Me among Nereids: lonely Poseidon
Will likewise lean and listen with a deep-sea stare
To his fan-mail crackling
In my hair.

P.S. I've never put to sea.
I live in a tower block in SE23.

A Clubman's Ozymandias

So this chap tells this other chap
Some damned clap-trap
About how somewhere on the old map
He's seen these de-bagged legs, and to cap
It all, not a scrap
On top of them, bugger all on tap
But the desert sands and similar pap –
Just a bloody great gap –
And the owner, poor sap,
Has had stencilled under the whole mishap
How one and all should funk and flap
Re his efforts: I mean to say, what crap!

Poetry

When they say
That every day
Men die miserably without it:
I doubt it.

I have known several men and women
Replete with the stuff
Who died quite miserably
Enough.

And to hear of the human race's antennae!
Then I
Wonder what human race
They have in mind.
One of the poets I most admire
Is blind,
For instance. You wouldn't trust him
To lead you to the Gents:
Let alone through the future tense.

And unacknowledged legislators!
How's that for insane afflatus?
Not one I've met
Is the sort of bore
To wish to draft a law.

No,

I like what vamped me
In my youth:
Tune, argument,
Colour, truth.

Moorhouse

Vaguely Australian rural North Kentish accents
Were still to be heard when I was a child
Before that music fell from the wires

And universal flatter South London took wing
Over the beechwoods, the downland lanes,
Brackened hillsides of fiddlehead ferns,

The flint in the chalk and the chalk in the clay-grey
Ploughland. By country bus-stops
After the war men singly stood,

A wiry crest on the regimental blazer,
The macintosh over the arm, the head
Brylcreemed or brilliantined on summer evenings,

Bound for pints of mild in the British Legion.
Kindly they were, as I recall,
These roll-up makers from deep scarred tins,

To me and my brother, two long-legged oddities,
Posh and animated and shy,
The boys who lived in the private school on the hill.

One thing we had in common was that we were poorish:
That and cricket. In the soap-box pavilion
Smelling of linseed oil and manhood,

My father said, 'Who are we playing next week?'
'Ideal, Ronnie.' 'I'm sure it is, Ivor,
But who are we playing?' Ide Hill was the answer

After more puzzled exchanges. A witless old man
Called Reg, still with thick black hair,
Cackled at the proceedings from the boundary,

Half in and half out of the trees. In their shade
Round-armed women in ample frocks
Made sandwiches. Behind them

The Austins 7 and 10 and the half-timbered shooting-brake
Clustered in the rutted copse. The field
Is wilderness now like the underbrush on the hillside

Where the lost balls nest forever, the pitch
(Much moss on it in its bouncing days
Over a bed of flint)

Sapped of all danger. I see my long-dead father
Pivot in thigh-high grass to hook
Hard and high into now where the ball dissolves

With the Kentish voices in their time of day.

Star and Garter

Alcoholic *Alma Mater*
Was for me the Star and Garter,
Country high street, suns ago,
Where I learned the Boozers' Charter,
Where, like infanthood of Sparta
(On the mountain, die or grow),

I was left (myself the dumper)
Either to become a Bumper
Jumbo Drunkard or again,
Not. It seems I chose the former,
Opting for Young's Winter Warmer,
Very favoured tipple then.

Anyway, the joint was slumping
As the denizens were stumping
Slowly up for pints and shots
One beige evening of late summer
Not-quite-rain was making glummer
Round us silent soaks and sots

When I caught a brittle chortle
From a gulched and ancient mortal
Crouching in a window seat
(With a bottled Guinness by her
Poverty could not deny her
And a mongrel at her feet),

Volunteering information
Of a bygone copulation,
Of a spectral intercourse:

'My husband
Was hung
Like a horse.'

As we turned, the self-same source
Cackled with redoubled force:

'My husband
Was hung like a
HORSE!'

What was this? Against the skyline
Broom-like poplars brushed their by-line
Under news and views of dusk
While inside that stagnant tap-room,
Limbs no longer giving sap room,
Croaked again this winnowed husk—

Ochre teeth like Sussex gorse—

'My husband
Was hung
Like a horse.'

Stools were swivelled. On that listening,
Unlit chandeliers were glistening.
'Who was *he*?' all wheeled and cried,
But the crone in rags but rich in
Memory unpicked no stitch in
Finer detail but replied,

Tapping out that self-same Morse:

'My husband
Was hung
Like a horse.'

And no word more. We failed to wheedle,
Howsoever logodaedal,
Further features of this spouse:
Crucially, of questions *seven*,
Was his mansion now in heaven
Or among the quick his house?

Was it death or just divorce?

My–

Two. What was his name? Three. Station?
Four. His worldly occupation?
Five. TT or on the sauce?
Six. If you don't mind confessing,
Was it more a curse or blessing?
Last. His nature, bland or coarse?

My–

Nix. Within the Star and Garter
I'm no more *persona grata*
Since it burned down, suns ago.
She, dog, equine attribution,
Wallow in the last solution
Far away upon the flow.

Down the rank and lonely mileage,
Through the lanes of stinking sileage

Of turned time, in single file
Here we come, but recollecting
In among the light-detecting
Instants, that which made us smile.

CRY OUT WHAT THE STARS ENDORSE:

Her husband
Was hung
Like a horse.

Victorian Family Photograph

Here is the mother all boobed and bodicey
Who started the children upon their odyssey.

There sits the father stern as a rock
Who rules the world with his iron cock.

Those the two children white as mice
Who saw the ghost in the attic, twice.

And who are we to suppose this vignette
Not threaded with love like a string quartet?

Neighbours

I first noticed the neighbours were getting smaller
When driving away, he had to stand
To put his foot on the clutch.
She leant on tiptoe,
Getting the rubbish into the garbage bin.

That evening, returning from work,
He set his shoulder to his briefcase,
Scraping it up the garden path
And reached to the heavens with his house-key.

Later we heard through the kitchen wall
Their quarrels like kittens mewing for milk.

Later we heard through the bedroom wall
Their tiny cries of love like cries for help.

Soon we'd be putting out birdseed for them:
But who was I to intervene?
For I was growing longer, day by night.

When I shaved
In the nude
In the morning,
The mirror reflected the wrong hair.
Soon I slept with my head up the chimney,
Feet out the window,
And outfaced the treetops, tip to tip.

And when it changed and I grew lower,
My chin on the basin, chest at the lavatory top,
And my voice grew slower and weaker

And lesser as theirs grew louder
In sudden authority with their new-found height,

I prayed they would do me no harm
As I had done them no harm,
Nor tread on a neighbour in or out of sight.

Letter to Anna, Pregnant

When I consider
By the frozen river
How we two shall never
Down some of these days
Meet in loving
Upon the ungrieving
Bank in forgiving
New-made rays

Of April sunlight
When touch is leaf-light
And love is outright
And darkness done,
Then I remember
Times without number
The cold I shouldered
To block your sun.

And I apportion,
By this sad station
Where ice to the ocean
Flows downstream,
All blame attendant
To your correspondent,
Sorrow his tenant,
Drowned that dream.

The hawthorn crouches
In the black wind's clutches
And snags and scratches
The last of light
That is dying over
The winter river
That sails forever
On out of sight.

I'm sorry, darling,
I hope the unfurling
Bud in your sailing
Body may
Beyond shores woeful
Wake you joyful,
Wake you joyful
Some sweet day.

Aubade

Disbelieving eyes
That love had kindled
Saw to their surprise

Love dwindled:

Everything they made
Not so much betrayed
As swindled.

Pity About Cleitus

Alexander the Great,
it says in my Oxford Junior Encyclopaedia,
'never forgave himself for killing
his best friend Cleitus by hurling a javelin
at him
at a

banquet.' Now there we see
how wounding a moment's thoughtlessness
to a loved one
can be.

  Myself,
if I ever ended the world with a nuclear bomb
in however fleeting a fit of pique,
I'd never forgive myself, reader.
It would live with me *all my life*.
But for me,

better yet to avoid these banquets.
That man at the end of the table, for instance,
the one with the Hitler moustache,
is Hitler, I'm sorry to say. And beside him the Khans,
Genghis and Elspeth, and little Attila
has come along with his hundreds of sons
and Huns.

Lay that javelin down, momma.
Pack up the blood and the meat.
They're all in your head. Don't give them

a thing to eat.

Mist on the Vine

The red vine twined in the apple boughs of October;
The infinitesimal spray of the mist that breaks
On leaf-edge, on lip, in eycs that will no more remember
Than tongue can answer the sad salt-carrying voices
Thrown by the overgrown garden's one slow grey breaker:
Though faithful lobelia and ox-eyed daisy persist
In the cracks, as it were, of the sea-cliff and one yellow rose
Swings like a lamp in the wind at the edge of the world . . .

They're a garden like one of those huge sea-reasoned hotels
Called the Metropole or the Grand that were so, in their time,
But resemble beached liners themselves or ships on the
ocean's
Floor; long-drowned
With the maritime baritone, downed with the deep-sea
barber,
The Nautical Question Time and the Ball in the Ballroom,
The lost excited voices of travelling children
Whom seaweed garlands, the vine on the apple-tree boughs.

Short Afternoons

Who would suppose a dryad in a laburnum
Accusing over a privet hedge? Or the woman
Who asks me the way and stares deep in my eyes
As though reading an autocue in them?
But we have entered

The country of short afternoons where every angle
Is filled with intense implication. Brickwork is pertinent,
Sycamore leaves
The wind scrapes widdershins over the pavement
Are freighted with dangerous meaning, a world

At your two-timing feet and its secret truth on the tip
Of your tongue. In the sky
A vapour trail is a pipe-cleaner metamorphosing
Into a papery silver birch limb, changing
Into a spoilage into the lake of darkness,

Sun knowing sudden
Disgrace as it falls from the arms of the tree of heaven.
And then the silver,
Black and too purple
Frieze is under vindictive construction,

Wind in its element again
Of Chaos and old night. So faces
That dip after work into pubs on the Holloway Road
Are electrical, tripped
Into such sudden transparency,

Into such lit significance there is reason
To fear and cherish, to huddle and talk excitedly,
Naming each others' names, since faces
Are offered once only, says the wind,
And the singable circumstance is being alive.

The Man of Distinction

(St Mary Abbots Hospital, Kensington, psychiatric wing)

Where speechfolk with most disparate cries
addressed the loosest possible agenda,

or null with drugs, slumped over tables,
the horror backed behind the face,

one there was, silent was,
admitted to that company:

a man of distinction, it was whispered,
not in those words. A male nurse told me

he had the CBE. An elderly
number in loosest possible hospital issue

dressing gown, he veered with a cane
or sat appalled in the day room. He'd

no family, no clothes, no short-term
memory, he couldn't recall

where his bed was, the place to piss,
or anything much but his name he spoke

in the loosest possible manner of speaking,
a quailing proposition, rather than

fact, poor one. Pale breath, his face
was nonetheless indeed distinguished:

an eagle head upon a forsaken body
and soul, tipped, bladed nose

and ruined eyes like splintered flint
wondering what had brought him to this pass

or made these things to be.

Later I found out who he was
and the field of his distinction:

psychiatry.

An Interview and After

The interviewer seems to be on the point
of sniggering at the subtle fair-mindedness
of his own line of questioning.
'Note,' he says,
'I do *not* ask you .. . ' (mouth corners twitching,
the tip of a shoulder pulsing) '. . . about the *some*thing,
but about the something *else*.' Which is almost
too much for him. Yet the Minister

has more than enough composure for two
and as it happens he owns as well
one of those languid/abrasive
smiling/fuck you voices they give out as prizes
at certain political seminaries. He replies:

at the sharp end in the medium term
on a one-off basis, bottoming out at the downturn,
the seedcorn's track record's interface
with the ro-ro big bang walkabout aside,
the sharp end *is* the medium term
and I think we might have got it
about right.

Now both these everymen
must surely lead intricate, difficult lives,
seamed, I presume, with personal sorrow,
hope and delight,
love that might never quite find its likeness,
the great and the little dismays
and, most likely, children
small or tall and revised self:
child of the days.

But you wouldn't guess it. Nor would you find it
at recent party ward meetings where the best
seem full of passionate self-righteousness,
pretending
people are not faceted
(none in the same light lies long),
that if only we could perfect
the notes of our song
no-one would die and nothing ever go wrong.

How the Wild South East was Lost

for Robert Maclean

See, I was raised on the wild side, border country,
Kent 'n' Surrey, a spit from the country line,
An' they bring me up in a prep school over the canyon:
Weren't no irregular verb I couldn't call mine.

Them days, I seen oldtimers set in the ranch-house
(Talkin' 'bout J. 'Boy' Hobbs and Pat C. Hendren)
Blow a man clean away with a Greek optative,
Scripture test, or a sprig o' that rho-do-dendron.

Hard pedallin' country, stranger, flint 'n' chalkface,
Evergreen needles, acorns an' beechmast shells,
But atop that old lone pine you could squint clean over
To the dome o' the Chamber o' Commerce in Tunbridge
Wells.

Yep, I was raised in them changeable weather conditions:
I seen 'em, afternoon of a sunny dawn,
Clack up the deck chairs, bolt for the back French windows
When they bin drinkin' that strong tea on the lawn.

In a cloud o' pipesmoke rollin' there over the canyon,
Book-larned me up that Minor Scholarship stuff:
Bent my back to that in-between innings light roller
And life weren't easy. And that's why I'm so tough.

Worried Man Blues

I was in a skiffle group
In 1959,
One chord to a line,
We were doing

Fine,

Playing *Worried Man* upon
The Hurst Green Church Hall stage,
Fifteen years of age
When Lonnie was

The rage,

Tea-chest bass and washboard and
Two three-chord tricks:
Somehow
No worries then:

My God I'm worried now.

George Herbert's Other Self in Africa

Thinking another way
  To tilt the prism,
I vowed to turn to light
  My tenebrism
  And serve not night
    But day.

Surely, I cried, the sieves
  Of love shake slow
But even. Love subsists
  Though pressed most low:
  As it exists,
    Forgives.

But my stern godlessness
  Rose through the sun,
Admonished me: Fat heart,
  So starving's fun?
  Whom have they art
    To bless?

Thereat my false thought froze,
  Seeing how plain
The field was where they died,
  How sealed their pain,
  And I replied,
    God knows.

And They Stoned Stephen

Acts 7.59

When Steve was a waddling toddler,
His Dad said, 'Counter attack!
If they ever start throwing stones at you,
Stone the buggers right back.'

But of course there were far too many.
He tried but they'd got all the clout
When they took out Stephen and stoned him,
When they stoned him, and took him out.

The Ridge

I cannot rationalise
the fear I feel by our apple trees
on the dark ridge between seasons,

nor explain why a serious child
in pedagogic sunlight unfolding
the mystery of a natural law
to a younger one, so
tranquillises.

Or the quickening inhalation
of autumn after the stopped breath
of summer in whose deceived garden
the high wall stands with the playground
laughing behind its back,

proffering yellow buds
of clematis and the old man's beard
of clematis, fearfully,
at once,

though the iron is in the green
and the night in the green's shadow
and everything watched by a near eye
that doesn't know
it's dead.

Let the gold and the wisdom begin.

Bloody Drama

(on the play *Bloody Poetry* by Howard Brenton at Hampstead Theatre)

I have to tell you plainly, Mr Brenton,
That though I liked the premise of your play
And took, I think, its points, the way it went on
Entombed me in a lonelier dismay
Than if I'd spent the evening out at Prenton
Park and watched Crewe Alex draw, away,
With Tranmere Rovers, nil-nil, in the rain.
I'm glad I went. I shall not go again.

The premise? Plays do not have premises,
I know, except a stage, or overweight
With programme, they'd be their own Nemeses
And kill themselves. No plan but to *create*
For splintered truth a pointed diadem, as is
The case with these sad laurels you fixate
Upon the mind of poetry. O.K.,
I see I am already miles away

From any point I was about to make
But that's a hazard of *ottava rima*,
A form I follow, flailing in the wake
Of him you cast as drunkard to your dreamer,
Byron to Shelley; thus you have them take
The boards. No premise then. And yet as schemer
Of this production I emerged so glum from,
You're canny in the angle that you come from.

It is the minor figures in the *coterie*
That draw your bitter interest. So far,
So excellent. That Bysshe, the Super Votary
Of airy revolution, lived to scar
His acolytes on earth, you, zealous notary,
Notate with nous for where the hurt things are:
The unreality that got him plastered
Meant dreamy Bysshe was something of a bastard

In personal terms. And are there any others?
Is there authentic love that grows beyond
Immediates? To quite whom were they brothers,
These frenzied aristos? *One's* strongest bond,
It might seem, was with self: cold self that smothers
Love and dumps a dead wife in a pond.
Like any John and Jane or Dai and Blodwen,
The loves of Bysshe, though, and of Mary Godwin

Or his for Harriet, hers for him, remain
Opaque for ever and survive as mystery,
Lonesome secrets washed out by the rain
Filling the sea of European history
That will not, either, wash to shore again
The truth of Byron's fling with his half-sister. He
Leaves prurient posterity to muster
Half-lies about half-love. As does Augusta.

Such famous ghosts cannot be insulated,
However, from surmise, I quite agree.
But something in your treatment of them grated:
Too sure, too crude, too shrill, it seemed to me.
I felt their spirits had been violated.
My second, more specific beef, Beef B—
Lest that objection seem too vague and dopey:
Some of the dialogue was rather ropey.

The text, though you were properly reliant
On quoted verse and prose, was not believable
At many points, and each poetic giant
Had things to say I thought were inconceivable.
Too many clichés. Still, if I say, 'Why aren't
Their lines the goods?' it's damned hard, if achievable,
To verbalise a man who, when not dreaming,
May well have spent so much spare time in screaming.

His writing, though. Harsh years it took to do it
And this is why your play has made me sad—
The reason also why there's so much to it,
Such point and anguish: Shelley's songflame had
As aim to burn the dark world and renew it
Whole. It didn't. Doesn't. That's as mad
And blind as when he started. The malaise
Is poems don't change systems. Nor do plays.

The Old of Today

Don't worry about the old.

The past is in safe hands.

They've got their heads
Screwed firmly to the ground
And wise feet
On their shoulders.

Don't worry about the old.

They know which side they're battered.
They can crack it, joint by joint,
They can carry
The baton
Back.

Have confidence in the old.

They know what they're doing, the Main
Chance they see
Leaves nothing
To chance
And they suss which way
The wind is blowing
In and out of their bones.

Believe in the old

As they believed in you, it's
Their turn now
To dream their future

Like nothing on God's earth,
To hoist
Their black sail on the Enid Blyton
Sea of Adventure
Into the bay

Where long-beaked gulls
Assemble.

Encourage the old.

They can cut the mustard.

Relax. Just
Leave it to them.

The Burden of the Mystery

It's a strange afternoon's rugby, one player
To a couple of teams of referees,
For the dead outnumber the living
By thirty to one.

That's thirty slow shadow dancers
Round a lit candle,

That's the radiating hub of a many-spoked wheel
And the stamen in the corolla's heart
That forms the inflorescence.

The small craft ploughing toward the harbour lights.

Comeback

(The last and retired executioner spends a day on location advising on a hanging scene in a film. At the end of it the director thanks him. He replies: 'Thank *you* . . . it's been a long time.')

When a hangman hangs up his noose
And retires from the game,
He can think he's of little use,
A forgotten name,
A hasbeen deathshead, a snuffed-
Out old hellflame,

A superannuated
Extinction bore,
Lonely and dumb and dated,
Shoved out the door
By new and pacific fashions,
A dinosaur.

When an executioner bites
The dust of old age,
He sees himself, by his lights,
A turned-over page
Of history that discards
A Killing sage.

But when a movie unreels
In someone's brain
And they ask him his know-how he feels
His oats again!
Back on the tried old track
Of the State-slain.

Back with the dear old Sentence—
He knows the tropes!
Back with the priest's attendance—
Best of Soaps!
Back with the expertise—
He knows the ropes!

So when a hangman returns
And hangs up his hat
Near where his warm fire burns,
He's the better for that—
Keeping his horrible hand in,
And hearing the chat.

Ecclesiastical History

(the anagrammatised *Poetry Review*)

Eve (prey or wit?)
Ever wore pity.

Tie every prow
To weepy river,

To weepy river
Rope every wit.

Rev wore piety.
RIOT EVERY PEW!

The Sub-Song

for Richard Mabey

I thought it a piece of fancifulness
when first I heard it mentioned:

the sub-song of the wintering bird:

but no, it's a scientific
classification of sound, denoting

a drowsily territorial
foreshadow, rehearsal or update,

sung past the leafless tree
in a minor key.

With no particular
dedicatee.

Or recitatif between arias,
summer and summer,

song of the slumbering, fixate
middle-comer.

I think I have caught the sub-song sounded
in various winter bars

by singletons with their beaks buried under

their shoulders, or in supermarkets,
wobbling alone a trolley,

with one wheel
out of true:

far from the buzzard's mew
or the squawk of hawk on wrist,

crying, I fly, I can sing, I am here, I exist,
perpetually,

but it might have been nothing, or there again,
might have been me.

Unlikely Obbligato of Andersonstown

for Liam Parker

'O short shrift's the best shrift to give to this *Festschrift*!'
The poor old Professor moaned, citing reviews
Of the tome in his 'honour' but lighting upon her
Has changed his estrangement and made him enthuse:

'As right as a trivet and neater than privet,
As white and as light as the snow milling down,
O she is the rarest and likewise the fairest
That ever went walking through Andersonstown.'

Dispraise universal at read-through, rehearsal
And scunnered short run meant the elderly ham
Was half suicidal but viewing his idol
Has swivelled his snivel to *Cherchez la Femme*.

'O hear my hosanna! Eyes blue as Fermanagh,
Where any old-stager might happily drown,
And bright as the sun on the water, that daughter,
The loveliest ever in Andersonstown.'

The stricken logician reviewed his position.
He couldn't decide if he was or was not,
With nothing to go on but so forth and so on
And so forth. Her beauty has taught him what's what.

'O through the mind's mazes, let ring out her praises,
Though bombs they go up as the bullets come down,
Her loveliness one shot that's cleaner than gunshot
That ever went flying through Andersonstown.'

So let it be re-capped. O never be knee-capped:
If you're not the queen of it, I am the clown.
Take care of your beauty: that's only your duty
To three poor sods stomping through Andersonstown.

Monarch as Irishman: A Racial Cliché

Her Majesty Queen Elizabeth the Seventh
Was a lovable rogue:
Always landing in the shit
And charming her way out of it
With her Windsor brogue.

This scalliwag Queen Elizabeth the Seventh
At Sandringham Fair,
The worse for a glass of parsnip wine,
Is up to her usual tricks. The line
She's selling there

Is damned little dogs called Corgis, if you please,
And here's the slyness:
They've only three legs and that's the ramp
Of your man, this lovable no-good scamp,
Her Royal Highness.

And this is the beauty of the business, sound affair,
The Sovereign's disguised!
Blow me down if she hasn't got
Her headscarf back to front so's not
To be recognised!

Trade's brisk enough for this divilish Defender of the Faith
And O'Malley, the fool,
Is next in line to pay good cash
For a class of a barking tripod trash–
A yapping *stool*!

When out of the rain up staggers the Lord Chief Justice,
Soaked to his vest,
And cries out: 'Sovereign of sea and strand,
Monarch of air and wave and land—
You're under arrest!'

But here is your Royal cuteness. Quick as you like,
'It seems,' says she,
'Four threes are twelve and so's three fours,
I'll give you a dozen damned little paws
For the price of three!'

Yes. Her Majesty Queen Elizabeth the Seventh
Was a lovable rogue:
Always landing in the shit
And charming her way out of it
With her Windsor brogue.

Found Among His Papers

An end to all twitting and taradiddle.
Head and shoulders below the rest,

My art had beginning and ending but never a middle,
Existed simply to attest

There's many a vile tune played on an old, croaked fiddle
And many a false word spoken in jest.

Lead Like Leather

(to the direct metal sculpture, 'Harness', by Peter Greenslade)

That lead should wear the muted sheen
  Of working country leather, laid
At rest upon a barn floor, mean
  The same slow-motion cavalcade
Of strap and buckle, seems to me
  Triumphant in a simile.

I rub the leather's molten grain
  And smell the linseed in the lead.
The soft Convergence of the Twain
  Sinks pleasure deep inside my head:
I like it that the world should be
  So veined with similarity,

  All men, all things be family.